♥ For the Animals,
may our hearts remember your sacredness
and be open in safety to you.

Clarion Books is an imprint of HarperCollins Publishers.

Sanctuary

www.harpercollinschildrens.com

ISBN 978-0-35-820543-2

The artist used graphite, watercolor, acrylic, and digital paint to create the illustrations for this book.

Typography by Julia Denos and Celeste Knudsen

22 23 24 25 26 RTLO 10 9 8 7 6 5 4 3 2 1

First Edition

Sanctuary

A Home for Rescued Farm Animals

words and pictures by

Julia DeNos

CLARION BOOKS

An Imprint of HarperCollins*Publishers*

It is dark, but I can see your light.

You are afraid, but I am here.

And here you are safe.

Here you have a name, instead of a number —
because you and I are friends.

You are some*one*,

and not some*thing*.

Here is home. Where you can be
who you were born to be, just like me.

Let's feel the earth, stretch our legs,
lift our hooves, and spread our wings!

Here your value comes
from being you —

not the milk and cheese you
were forced to make . . .

not your eggs, or your babies,
or the meat that they take . . .

No.

Here your body is safe.

Your family is safe.

Your heart is safe, in mine.

You can trust my hands
to help you heal.

You can rest and grow old.
Here you can dream a deep dream.

For, you and I,
we both dream indeed.

Grownups think I'm too young
and small to understand.

But I don't need to grow up to know . . .

That I love you and
want to protect you, and
that will never change.

That your light and my light
are the same.

That I am in charge of my own heart,

and my two arms are open wide.

And it is all I need to make

a place for love to live inside.

Where my love is safe in you,

and your love is safe in me.

I can be your sanctuary.

Dear Caregiver,

When we connect with an animal, it's a powerful thing. A bond of trust forms and awakens our human instincts to nurture and protect: we become a safe place for love. Children know this best.

For we are born knowing, without anyone teaching it to us—before society, culture, or advertising convinces us otherwise—that our connection to animals is sacred. But as we grow, our instinct to love animals becomes divided among species. We are taught that only *some* of these trusting, thinking, feeling beings, like our domesticated dogs and cats, are worthy of the laws and rights that come with love—consent, bodily autonomy, safety—while *other* domesticated animals, "farm animals," are not.

Instead, we are taught that farm animals are not individuals. They have numbers punched through their ears or spray-painted onto their bodies. They are taken from their families and sold at auctions like merchandise. They are often transported long distances to slaughter and exposed to the elements in metal livestock trailers on the highway. And while we care for our pets like family, we are taught that farm animals exist only for our consumption, so it is normalized to violate and exploit their bodies, while disrespecting their social bonds and ending their lives at a fraction of their natural life spans. It is standard practice that mothers and babies are separated and that they lose their lives in order to maintain a continual supply of milk, cheese, beef, and bacon. Male chicks, considered an unwanted byproduct of the egg industry, are killed at just one day old by the hundreds of millions each year in the United States alone. This brutality is strategically hidden from us. Why?

Because if we looked with our hearts, as children do, so much would have to change in order to reflect justice for animals, people, and our planet. Because when we visit a sanctuary and look into the eyes of a dairy cow, there is no question. She plays, cuddles, and licks to show her affection, just like our dogs do. We know, with our sacred knowing, she is no object.

Speciesism has done more than just teach us to divide our love from animal to animal; it has normalized dividing our actions from the

*Can you identify the wild plants in this book? Look for dandelion, garlic mustard, ground ivy, horseweed, milkweed, mullein, red clover, white clover, and plantain. Can you spot the pollinators around them?

empathy, integrity, and truth of our hearts. On a larger scale, it has distanced us from the natural world and built disconnected food systems, which harm the environment and lack healthy, compassionate, accessible, and sustainable ways to feed our human family. I painted these pictures to reconnect us. To reimagine, together. To open the book to a *bigger* healing picture, perhaps: one in which "sanctuary" could mean rehabilitating our connection to the earth and all its inhabitants, through restoring native habitats and species, to expanding education on plant-based nutrition, to widening access to locally foraged and cultivated foods.

A big picture always starts small, with love. For to be transformed by love is to transform the whole world.

Small ways you can make big changes:

- Take a tour at an animal sanctuary near you and learn the stories of the rescued animals who live there.
- Volunteer at a community vegetable garden, or start your own in a pot.
- Plant a native perennial to provide food and shelter for native species.
- Learn about simple nutrient-dense plant foods accessible to you.
- Check out a vegan cookbook from the library and try a recipe, or make your favorite dish with a friend, swapping in plant-based ingredients.
- Advocate for animal rights, farmworkers' rights, and environmental rights
- Draw your dream of a world where animals, people, and the planet are loved and respected.

I'll be dreaming with you.

Julia